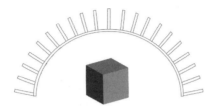

The Book Of The Recorder

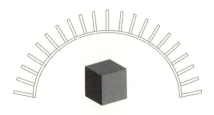

The Book Of The Recorder

Written by NATLO2

Transcribed by Dk 2

Released & Approved by the USD of AlnR

Rutledge Books, Inc.   Danbury, CT

ALL RIGHTS RESERVED
Rutledge Books, Inc.
107 Mill Plain Road, Danbury, CT 06811
1-800-278-8533
www.rutledgebooks.com

Manufactured in the United States of America

Cataloging in Publication Data
GERLACK

The Book of the Recorder

ISBN: 1-58244-167-7

1. Fiction.

Library of Congress Control Number: 2002100351

TABLE OF CONTENTS

INTRODUCTION

This book reveals the interpretation of what is probably the most significant archaeological find in the history of mankind. It provides some answers to events that took place thousands of years ago when man first inhabited this earth, and gives an insight into changes that may take place years into the future as man progresses. Such major changes as:

1. eliminating the use of and need for money,
2. eliminating marriage to establish total independence and equality,
3. eliminating organized religion and allowing each individual to develop his own beliefs of the two unknowns,

are discussed here along with the structure and philosophy of this advanced civilization. The information presented here completely changes how man will forever look at his past and his role in the future.

The discovery of this information took place in 1958 A.D. following a storm off the east coast of Florida. It was here that a diver, at a depth of approximately eighty feet of water, found what appeared to be a tightly lashed black cube. Upon further examination of this cube, it actually was found to be a stack of very thin flexible ceramic sheets, each of which was entirely covered with a black coating. With the use of some type of scribing tool, the black surface was removed leaving a permanent etched record of figures and symbols to be viewed by future generations.

The significance of this find was immediately realized by the diving team and the writings were taken to Washington D.C. for further investigation. It has now been forty years since the discovery of the cube, and only now is some information being released. A scientific team was assigned the job of encoding the strange writings which proved to be more complex than ancient hieroglyphics. Finally, within the last ten years, with the advancement of modern computer capacities and numerical-figural logic, an interpretation was achieved. Much of the information is still classified and work continues in Washington where the writings are kept, but the small portions that have been released are presented here revealing an incredible past and a possible future.

Using modern day dating techniques, it was determined that these writings were made about 10,000 years ago by a man named Natloz. Believing he was the last survivor of an advanced civilization, he wanted to leave a record of its history and existence to peoples of the future. Upon completion of these writings, he bound them together and awaited his fate. His location was on a beach on the east coast of Florida which later became submerged in water following the Ice Age. It was here that the writings were found and where search still continues in the hope of finding other material objects.

This translation of the Natloz writings is an attempt to present the "story" as written by Natloz in his exact words and meaning. Of course it involves some interpretation of time and distance for a comparison to be made with present day units; but, those involved with the project believe these values to be correct as given. Any notes and titles that have been added to these writings for the purpose of clarification are enclosed with parentheses ( ) to separate them from the original writings. With this understanding, we present these fascinating writings (that have become known as "the Book of the Recorder") along with the question to all who read this book—ARE WE, THE DESCENDANTS OF THIS EARLY CIVILIZATION, REALLY THE ALIENS ON PLANET EARTH?

Dk Z
2000

THE END OF THE BEGINNING

38*300. It appears I may be the last survivor of what was the center of the most advanced civilization in this corner of our galaxy. If this is true, I feel it is my duty to leave as detailed a record as possible of the history of this civilization and of the accomplishments our people achieved. Although I am but one individual with a limited amount of time, I realize that any information I can pass down to future generations will be useful. It is a fact that you can learn from history and, by taking the best from the past, you can avoid mistakes in the future.

My people arrived here approximately 40,000 to 50,000 years ago after traveling through space for almost a full generation. We came from a planetary system whose life cycle was coming to an end. Even with our superior knowledge and control of our own environment, it was impossible to stop the coming disaster, the collision of our planetary system with that of another star. It was possible to predict this collision hundreds of years in advance thereby allowing time to prepare for the only solution—evacuation.

A maximum effort was made to locate a planetary system

that was within seventy-five light years of our home planet, and one capable of sustaining our life-forms. This meant a planet that was approximately the same size as ours so gravity would not take its toll on our bodies; and one with water, oxygen, and a similar temperature. The distant limit of seventy-five light years was chosen for practical reasons. With our typical life span of up to 150 years, it permitted someone with experience from our home planet to help establish the new colony and not rely on those whose entire life was spent on a spacecraft. Also a hundred years was the estimated limit of how long a fully loaded spacecraft could maintain the life of its inhabitants. Although near 100% recycling of our materials was possible, a small amount of our natural resources and supplies was lost in energy traveling through space. Perpetual motion could not be achieved.

It should be mentioned that in the very early years of our planetary research, much time was wasted trying to contact other advanced civilizations in our universe. When fantasy and unrealistic imagination finally gave in to the practical speed limits of space travel, the whole philosophy of scientific research changed. Even as the speed of our spacecraft approached the theoretical limit, which was the speed of light, we realized the size of our universe ruled out the possibility of meeting another intelligent life form. By traveling at the speed of light, it would take 750,000 years to get to another galaxy or even 30,000 years just to reach the center of our own galaxy. Space communication takes the same length of time. If we could locate intelligent life as close as seventy-five light years away, it would take 150 years to get answers to any questions we had. This makes communication unpractical. We all accepted the realization that, because of the unimaginable size of the universe and the process of evolution, there was no doubt that other intelligent life existed even similar to our own. To meet them, however, was ruled out. This was a case where, although we knew there were others like us, our isolation required us to consider ourselves unique. For this reason, we were on our own.

By the time our unbearable environment made evacuation necessary, we had found five planetary systems within the critical distance of seventy-five light years that appeared to meet the requirements for our survival. It was decided to divide up the population into five groups since no one knew whether the exact conditions at the various destinations would allow a group to survive. In all cases it was a one way trip since a return trip would go well beyond the destruction time of our home planet.

Each group was fully equipped with all the necessities to make the trip, and, hopefully, everything needed for survival. Specialists in every field were included in every group along with a complete library of the recorded history and a knowledge of our civilization so it could be taught and passed down to future generations.

The group destined for this planet was the smallest in size since it was the farthest of the five destinations and there was only a limited number of advanced spacecraft large enough to make the journey. These advanced spacecraft were equipped with the special forward x-ray shields that were needed for protection against the "wall" effect as one approaches the speed of light. But, one can only hope that no major collision would occur once the course was set. The entire fleet consisted of twenty spacecraft with approximately 20,000 individuals at launch time.

Our group was the first to evacuate the doomed planet and we were given the designation "A" colony. The trip here to our new home was fortunately uneventful. What is important is that survival conditions here on this planet were near ideal. Its size was slightly smaller than our home planet, which meant our bone structure was stronger than needed and although its rotation between lightness and darkness was slightly faster than at our home planet, we knew we could adjust. Most important of all was the fact that its home star was located at just the right distance that the temperature of the planet was almost identical to the planet we left behind.

Upon arrival, the planet was completely surveyed and for natural protection an island 1500 units square located in a temperate climate was selected as the landing sight. The ideal conditions and location allowed for the rapid establishment of the colony. Large public buildings were raised, and canals and roadways were established. Huge energy generators were located over the water on the windward side of the island which boiled water for purification and also provided environmental control of the weather by making the mist needed for irrigation. The entire city complex was named Acol after the original fleet's designation as "A" colony.

But before I discuss the achievements of Acol, I would like to pass on to you a short history of what we were taught in school about the doomed planetary system my ancestors originally came from some 50,000 years ago. It was a highly developed civilization that had been in existence for almost 9000 years. It's people had solved the problems of poor health and eliminated diseases as new ones occurred. Aging was slowed down with life spans increasing to 150 years. All needs were supplied to each individual and life was considered very good. This, however, was not always the case.

Many centuries before this ideal state, the planet was divided into hundreds of individual political groups made up of different races and cultures. Each physical area had manmade boundaries that isolated and separated them. Since all wealth comes from nature and the environment, certain areas did not have the natural resources to sustain the people within those areas. Some of the areas would be rich in minerals, while other areas had fertile lands for growing food. Some had an abundance of fresh water, while others had a hostile environment. No political area was self-sufficient.

There was also a population problem. Even though the

people were very intelligent, it took years to achieve this ideal state, and by that time the planet was overpopulated. This resulted in food shortages in the smaller areas, and the draining of natural resources that could not be replaced even with a strong recycling program.

All of these conditions resulted in those that "have," and those that "have not." Peace could never be achieved as long as the political boundaries existed. War resulted from emotion, such as revenge, or when someone wanted something someone else had. It was always political and always a waste. War, whether you win or lose, are brave or fearful, still results in people dying. This was the case throughout the early development of our civilization.

Then an amazing thing happened. An uncontrollable plague covered the entire planet wiping out over ninety percent of the population. This happened over many years and the sky was filled with smoke from the millions of cremated victims. Surviving people throughout the world worked together to eliminate the plague and this began the unification of the planet.

To begin with, one of the largest and most technically advanced countries created a communication network. This resulted in the establishment of a common language where a given word meant the same to everyone. This country also had an abundance of manufactured products since they were not destroyed by the plague and ninety percent less population needed them. This resulted in the survivors having everything they needed and then some. The excess items were made available free to any country willing to join a common union under one political rule. Smaller countries could contribute by just providing a small labor force or by using their lands as living or resort areas. When it was all over, the organizing country was able to unify the peoples of the entire planet by peaceful means and with the approval of the people. A mini paradise was achieved. Since there were no political boundaries, the resources were accessible when needed to provided for the materialistic needs of all the people. The common language between all people resulted in continuous global communication which eliminated isolation and serious disagreements. With the needs of the people satisfied, the governing body was able to limit the population growth, provide education for all, eliminate health problems, and, above all, establish permanent peace. All these improvements took many many years. In the end, man demonstrated he could control man and make the best use of his surroundings, but he could not, however, dominate nature. There was nothing man could do to stop the collision of our planetary system with the oncoming star.

39*316. (restricted)

40*344. (restricted)

THE NEW WORLD DIVIDED

41*359. As I continue to sit here under dark skies, I keep trying to remember and record all I can since this history and information is so close to being lost forever.

When my ancestors first arrived on this planet, they were strong and healthy, and were able to adapt to their new environment quickly. They were all similar in physical appearance in that they all had dark black hair and a tan colored skin. This appearance resulted from the genes they developed over thousands of years of living together. With their arrival they brought with them all the knowledge of the advanced civilization they left behind, along with specialists in each field. Since they were limited as to how much equipment they could bring in the twenty spacecraft, their cargo was made up of only the tools needed to establish the colony and a few weapons for protection. It was up to them to find and develop the materials and food needed to survive.

After the location of Acol was established and the island was explored, minerals from around the planet were quickly located and stored as needed. It was easy to locate them with their orbiting spacecraft and advanced detecting equipment. After the minerals were located, they were mined and returned to Acol for storage. Then these outposts would be shut down until further needs arose. Once a sufficient excess of materials was achieved, there was little need for individuals to leave the island.

While mining and traveling around the globe, large physical signs and symbols were built so they could be seen from outer space. They were constructed to welcome any descendants from the other four colonies that left our original doomed planet. After all these years, however, we have never made contact with them and do not even know if they survived.

Other than the minerals and materials needed for construction, there was, of course, the need for food. Fortunately the grain and seeds that were brought on our colonizing ships flourished in this new world, and this food along with newly discovered foods was abundant.

For the record it should be mentioned that other primitive human forms were found scattered around this planet. They were well back in the evolutionary chain with a much smaller cranial size than ours. To them we were the unknown and considered evil gods. They were violent and, although we tried to avoid them, clashes occurred when some of our expeditions went ashore. Of course they were no competition for our modern weapons, and try as we may, we were never able to befriend any of them. For some reason over the next 10,000 years, this species of lower form humans disappeared from existence. It is our belief that they could not adapt to the warming climate at that time and the new diseases that were introduced because of this change.

With our people now the only survivors on this planet, an unplanned division occurred that has resulted in a continuing study of man for over 20,000 years. Every so often, individuals, or small groups of individuals, leave our island of Acol to live on the surrounding continents. These individuals may leave willingly because they need a greater challenge to their life than they experience on Acol, or they may actually be banished from Acol for not adhering to its rules. In either case, they must survive in the new world on their own without returning and we have made a continuous study of their progress with amazing observations.

The first people to leave Acol attempted to establish settlements on the surrounding continents that were similar to those left behind on the island. Even though they had the advanced knowledge and training they took with them, it was impossible to maintain traditional conditions without modern technology. Survival became the key issue and it was soon back to basic skills. Archaic weapons were developed along with baskets and pottery to be used for everyday needs. Cultivation for food along with herding of existing animals was established. Some of the early groups found living in caves to be the easiest and quickest way to establish quarters. Eventually all modern technology was lost.

Then very gradually over many generations, major changes were noted. Because of the hardships and new diseases, the natural lifespan of these individuals was greatly shortened. Their skin color began to change depending on where their settlement was located. Some became lighter while others were darker. Even their language changed to where it is now difficult to understand them. As different groups discovered new plants or animals or processes, they gave them new names which has resulted in many new languages further dividing those located in the wilderness.

But their greatest loss was the loss of the knowledge that had been accumulated over thousands of years. No matter how intelligent an individual is, he is totally dependent on others in society for help, and his advanced knowledge is useless in primitive surroundings. What good is it to be an expert in electronic devices when there are no advanced materials or individuals around to make them. Or what good is it to be an atomic physicist in a society where survival is the primary concern. All of this experience and knowledge is useless and lost in a non-technical society. Observing and studying these isolated settlements has actually shown us that the more technically advanced the individuals are when establishing a new settlement, the quicker it reverts to a more primitive society. As basic knowledge is lost from one generation to the next, physical laws and phenomena are no longer understood, and religion and superstition are once again introduced to explain the unknowns. More on this later.

About once every year, "gathering teams" from Acol were

sent out to obtain necessary supplies and to get further information on how these outer settlements were advancing. I was on the last ship out on one of these gathering missions when in the distance a huge explosion occurred and the sky darkened. I attempted to return to Acol but found no trace of the island. I have no idea what happened other than the large island had been totally replaced by water. For several months I searched for survivors but had no luck in even finding one. There are of course the various settlements around the planet, but they are hostile towards me since they had been ignored by the citizens of Acol and were left to survive by themselves without being allowed to return to Acol. For this reason we mutually avoided each other.

When my ship ran low on fuel, I selected an isolated beach to settle on to wait for possible survivors and to spend the rest of my days. I will continue my writing for as long as practical starting with information that is most important for an advanced civilization. The farther a civilization advances, the more technically dependent it becomes. These technical developments can be discussed to amaze and entertain the reader, but the information is useless without minute details of how these developments can be achieved. What is important is how an advanced civilization is socially organized to encourage individuals to be creative to develop new ideas. This ultimate society can be divided into five major areas for discussion. These are Religion, Education, Government, Science, and Social Life (including Work). I will attempt to cover each of these subjects in detail.

RELIGION AND A
PHILOSOPHY OF LIFE

42*372. I would like to start by discussing my knowledge of religion. Even though religious practices no longer exist in our advanced society, and even though religion has not played a part during my lifetime, I realize with the current situation it will once again be introduced to mankind and recycled in history to play a major role in its development.

Religion was important and useful to early civilizations. It was used to explain the unexplainable to peoples who did not yet understand natural science. Primitive societies were bound together with myth, superstition, and imagination, because of their inability to explain natural phenomena. Those individuals with their insight and ability to make use of nature, soon became the leaders of the people. Their knowledge of nature permitted them to predict obvious natural events and to perform miracles by healing with medications developed over the years. Since these individuals could not control nature, they established "all powerful spirits" or "gods" to perform and be responsible for these natural forces such as rain, wind, light, and darkness. These individuals became religious leaders and went by such titles as "prophets" or "priests." They acted as intermediaries between man and the gods.

Early civilizations had many gods. But, as each religion became more sophisticated, these civilizations ended up worshiping the same god without realizing it. Their God was the right God and the only God. God was the all powerful "Supreme Being" of infinite intelligence. At the same time, God was not a person, but an impersonal force in all that truly exists, and was interchangeable with "principle," "law," "being," "mind," and "spirit." Since no one actually knew what God was, God was simply defined as "everything," "infinite," and "eternal." God's activity on Earth was the "Holy Spirit." This invisible psychic force or divine energy was how God showed love and power.

As early religion progressed, ancient oral tradition was passed down by word of mouth from one generation to the next. But it became difficult to justify God without some "written word" to refer to. This resulted in the writings of "holy books" using the "words of God" passed down through some intermediary or prophet. Much of the writings were stories to teach the followers rules and morals, and were generally based on historical occurrences with inserted miracles and exaggerations. All holy books generally includes a common man, born of a virgin, who then evaded assassination, and as a child was intelligent beyond his years. This then ties God in with man. Other parts of the book can be violent, threatening, and usually includes laws sent from God. These books written by man and said to be the words of God, become the controlling laws people are to live by. Some fundamentalists actually tried to live exactly by the words as written while others interpreted the stories with different religious meanings. Neither makes sense since all "holy books" were written by man. This is obvious by the fact that old religious prophets restricted themselves to their present and had no insight about future conditions such as man flying in the heavens or conquering disease.

Although religion became a means of controlling the people primarily through fear, it also served the important function that gave these early individuals hope and a purpose to life. As with politics, religion promised the people everything they could desire such as good health and a rewarding life in the hereafter. This of course, was attainable only if they lived by the rules written in the holy books and did repentance and prayer for their mistakes. However amazing as it sounds, certain religions even allowed individuals to murder or rob others as long as they admitted their guilt to their religious leaders and said they were sorry for their actions.

People were told they were basically good, but fallible and needing guidance. The balance between their good deeds and bad deeds would determine the destiny of their souls or spirit. When the final day of reckoning and rewards came, the obedient and the forgiven would live forever in paradise with God, and the unrighteous would suffer. Those believing in reincarnation would be reborn to a better status or a worse suffering based on performance in their current life. All religions had the same principles and aims.

The poor and the sick masses took strongly to religion in that it taught that all souls are equal in the sight of God. It gave them a better feeling since they could do nothing about their status in life. The holy books told people to be kind and caring to the poor and oppressed, and that good causes happiness and evil causes pain and discomfort. Most religious educators and priests actually believed what they taught to others because that is what they themselves were taught. Very few made an effort to think for themselves and much of natural law had yet to be discovered. Any unexplainable variation from the norm, such as a mutation or self healing, was still considered a miracle.

For a religion to survive, many controls were used. They included 1)forcing one to marry only within their own religion thereby perpetuating the group; 2)requiring people to bring up their children in the same religion; 3)keeping to "the word" or fundamentalism, thereby resisting change (this is anti-modern); and 4)treating the religion as a family where the rulers (priests) were the adults and the people were the children.

Over the centuries, it turned out that more bad than good was accomplished by religion. Religion was a tool of oppression and became based on control and power. Rather than looking at the good in man, it stressed the evils of man. Thousands of people were killed or executed for opposing religious leaders. Different religions kept the world divided and wars and crusades were fought over pieces of dirt called "sacred" with "God" supporting both opponents.

Civilized men with "holy books" ruined and even eliminated slower cultures with disease and domination.

Religion also suppressed the individual and created herd morality. It taught that faith and rigorous adherence to doctrine, were all that man needed to fulfill his obligations during his lifetime, and everything would turn out for the best. Since this was the case and all would be well, people lost their incentive and drive to make the world a better place. Religion promoted selfish greed with most individuals praying for health, wealth, and salvation for themselves. Even a person's afterlife became more important than his present activities. In some religions, people just laid on the ground and starved saying it was "their karma" and to take what comes. In some cases the "God made me do it" defense was used when a person would no longer accept personal responsibility for his actions and needed an excuse. When problems became overwhelming, man became frustrated and lost his "free will" to make his own decisions. And, finally, there was the guilt feelings that were brought on by religion. Since religion taught there was a reason for everything, an individual that had poor health or a crop failure would begin to wonder what he had done wrong that God was punishing him. These all contributed to suppressing the individual.

One really should ask what contribution had religion made to the advancement of civilization. In actuality, it held advancement back. Science in a hundred years contributed more to civilization than religion did in thousands of years. Materialism sets no boundaries on knowledge, whereas spiritualism is an admission of ignorance and is based on the fear of the unknown.

With the advancement of science and knowledge of the universe, man eventually concluded that the only purpose for religion was to prepare man for life after death. This belief, along with the unification of all people with a common language, allowed for the establishment of a world religion. This world or "perfect religion" had five basic beliefs that were as follows:

1. There could only be one God. Since each old religion felt its god to be the strongest and most powerful, and since only one god could be the strongest and most powerful, it therefore must be the same god. This spiritual being was an invisible, impersonal power or force that was all intelligent, undefinable, and unknowable. God was unique and eternal.

2. This world religion had no one founder and was established by gathering input from all available religious leaders.

3. There was no "holy book" or "holy place". The "writings" of this religion were the selective gathering of all of the best writings of previous beliefs and religions.

4. The goal of this religion was to love one another, keep world peace, and achieve holistic health. This was to be accomplished through individual meditation to reach one's inner-self and not by group worship.

5. These goals were achievable through one's personal good works and behavior, not prayer. By showing patience

and compassion to one's fellow man, and by doing more good works then bad ones; one could achieve personal immortality.

Although it was through knowledge and communication that this world religion was established, these same two factors essentially eliminated organized religion altogether. In early times when hundreds of religions existed, they were prolonged by gathering into the "faith" individuals who were mostly uneducated and would go along with the crowd. The largest part of this group were the children led by their parents. A child does not question an adult or his parents and cannot reason for himself. An interesting fact was that ninety-five percent of the people were born into the "right" faith. This high percentage shows individuals did not question or study other religions, but just followed their parent's desires.

All of this changed as education became universal. Man was given the opportunity to use his brain (mind) to think and reason for himself, not just to accept what others told him. The more one knows of the physical world, the less of the unexplainable there is. Education eliminates unfounded beliefs and it is a fact that the more you learn and know, the less you have to believe. Knowing is the next step up from believing. For example, a person may believe his friend is innocent of a crime because he is such a good person, but in fact he does not actually know if his friend is innocent. To believe is to assume and accept as true, whereas to know is to understand based on facts.

For thousands of years, religious leaders asked people to <u>believe</u> in the unexplainable. They called them miracles. However, as communications improved and isolated areas were educated, miracles disappeared and could no longer be confirmed. God never again changed a physical law. God also quit appearing and talking to people. This common appearance in ancient times disappeared as people began to understand the physical world.

With the new world religion that was established, people did not believe God performed miracles or intervened in world events. At one time, people could not understand why an all knowing and powerful God would allow such worldly injustices as sickness, poverty, or the destruction of millions of people during wartime. When these events occurred, people concluded

1. God does not exist and hence cannot intervene,
2. God is not a good God,
3. God does not consider these events bad,
4. People do not know what is good or bad, or
5. God does not intervene in worldly events.

Originally, the standard answer was number four and religious leaders would tell the people "Who are we to know or question God's plan. We are nothing." With the new world religion, number five is now accepted and we know God has left us on our own.

One of the primary rules for the salvation of religion was to keep up with scientific advances and modern findings (such as evolution). Eventually, however, someone with a strong knowledge of science will find it difficult to be a religious person. Other than trying to explain where atoms originally came from, or what if anything happens after death, there is nothing else to explain. Science has explained and can create everything including life. For this reason there are those who do not believe in a personal spirit or afterlife, and just say life is over when its over. Then there are the other individuals who believe if you lead a good life, God will accept you as is, so why is there a need for religion. These two philosophies dominated religious thinking as the years progressed, and eventually there was no need for organized religion or theology. It was possible for an individual to believe in God without needing special guidance.

This elimination of organized religion did not occur gradually, but actually quite quickly following an elaborate study. This study consisted of selecting one hundred individuals that had various health problems, but without telling them of their selection. Then another group of several thousand individuals were organized to pray to God and ask Him to help with the healing of those one hundred individuals. The result was no different than praying to a stone. No improvement was noted. Then these same one hundred needy individuals were taught simple meditation and other positive thought techniques and an amazing 70% to 80% showed some improvement in their health. This study was repeated four more times with the results being near identical. From these results the following conclusions were made.

First it showed that group or organized praying was

ineffective. It was always this way but people wouldn't accept this fact. When they prayed and people got what they asked for - God was given the credit. If they didn't get what they prayed for, the people said it wasn't meant to be, but never blamed God. In other words what someone prayed for might happen or it might not. Either way God couldn't lose and got the credit.

Second it showed that praying for something or someone other than yourself was a waste of time. Whether by prayer or strong meditation, a person can only influence or get results on himself. Others have no control over another individual. God does not and must not get involved with everyday happenings so that man can be guaranteed his freedom and be responsible for his own actions and duties. Once man realized he was responsible for his own destiny, there was no limits as to what he could accomplish. In our society, all his material needs were met and eventually near perfect health was achieved resulting in a paradise here on earth. The concern was no longer preparing for the hereafter, but to get the most out of the present.

Happiness is the primary purpose of life and a goal of life is to know yourself. Understanding your own mind is to have awesome power and life provides you this opportunity. Only from within comes happiness, and it is the goal of each individual to provide himself inner peace. This self awareness can best be achieved through meditation and contemplation, with intellectual and creative pursuits providing the most happiness. It is mans' brain that separates him from other animals and allows him to utilize nature to create his needs and solve his problems. It is this creativity that provides his happiness. This creativity is not only in major achievements and the arts, but also in everyday life such as growing and planting the foods needed for life. The smallest achievements can provide as much happiness as the largest when each individual realizes his contribution is needed in society.

After many, many, thousands of years, man has finally realized and accepted the fact that it is up to himself to find a reason for his own existence, and not to rely on others for spiritual development. He has to decide for himself what is good, and not to rely on society. In fact it is not until he gives up worrying about what others think of him, that he can change his mind and discover truth. You must trust your own thoughts and not conform to your surroundings or have the need to be validated by others. This is best achieved by first expanding your own knowledge, and then through philosophical meditation that is best done when alone with nature. This replaces prayer and allows you to establish your own beliefs. The goal is to know one's self thereby achieving happiness and freedom. Enjoy the present.

Since the beginning of man, religion was used to explain the unexplainable. Finally only two questions were left unanswered. Where did matter come from, and where will it end up? It is impossible to justify something you can't explain. Even today there is still the group that just believes when life is over - its over. And then there is the second group that still believes there just has to be more to life after one dies. They believe in the spiritual world that we cannot get to in this life. Both groups however believe an individual should live and enjoy the present and not be concerned with something no-one knows anything about such as life after death. If there is a God which controls the hereafter, He must be good. And if one lives a good life, the results will be the same whether you believe in Him or not. If a day of reckoning comes, you are on your own and can't use personal references.

In the beginning God did not create man, but man created God because He was needed. Since then man has come to realize the only true thing man has control over is himself and that his body is only a temporary place. If an individuals life or spirit continues in some manner after death, only the contents of ones mind can be passed on. The body and anything physical remains behind. It is for this reason that man strives for knowledge and hopes to obtain peace of mind with his earthly desires and emotions. He also realizes that if he truly believes in this afterlife, only he himself can prepare for it. This individualistic approach was the root cause for the elimination of organized religion.

EDUCATION

43*397. *There is nothing more valuable to an individual than knowledge.* It gives power, removes superstition, develops independence, and in our society it determines how far one advances. Self awareness and knowledge allows you to become your own critic, your own philosopher, and to develop true wisdom. With these traits an individual can discover and develop new ideas and achieve the joy that comes from intellectual pursuits and contributions to society. After all, "happiness" is man's #1 goal in life.

To obtain knowledge you begin with education. Throughout history ignorance has been the root cause of all human suffering whether it was caused by those suffering or those in power. Without education one remains a slave since he is always dependent on others. Once educated, the knowledge remains with an individual and cannot be taken away. This human capital is more mobile than physical capital. Physical belongings can always be taken away from an individual, but what is in his mind remains.

Even though the state provides all the education needed to advance in society, it is up to the individual to take advantage of it. Having a book does not make one knowledgeable.

An individual must read and study that book to receive its benefits. It is the information in your mind that counts, but only if you can reason and use it. The more a person knows, the more chance he has of making the right decision when it is needed.

One then asks, what is the best way to teach an individual to allow him to attain his maximum capabilities? Since an individuals "mind set" is determined in the first ten years of ones' life, children must begin their formal education as soon as they begin to talk. This "mind set" carries one through life emotionally and determines one's creative drive.

Early in life care must be taken to teach children only facts and not something requiring reasoning. An individual cannot reason rationally without having sufficient data to base his conclusion on. This is why in ancient times something like a specific religion could be forced on a child since with his limited knowledge he would just accept it as fact. Afterwards it is difficult to change one's beliefs.

It is the goal of teaching to develop creative individuals that can make a contribution to society. To become a creative individual, one must not only have access to basic facts and information in his brain, but must also have a mind capable of organizing these facts to make them useful. This is accomplished by providing classes for learning to everyone throughout their entire life. It starts with the basics as a child and continues into old age when brain cleansing drugs are used to retard the build up and blockage of the brains mental channels. There is much to learn but also a lifetime to learn it.

Teaching and learning must be done in a logical, progressive sequence, so that an individual can develop his useful knowledge to maximum capacity. For example, an individual must first learn math skills before attempting to develop or use equations in physics. Over the years this optimum sequence for teaching has been perfected by our society.

Starting as a child, the primary subject to study and understand is how nature works. A better understanding of the laws of nature promotes a better understanding of man's destiny. To study nature, the child actually has half of his classes out of doors for his first eight years of schooling. Classes include the study of plants, animals, stars, weather, oceans, and in fact everything physical. Time is spent camping, doing environmental experiments, and planting gardens to learn how things grow. Everything is tied together to establish the importance of nature and how it effects each individual. This is a child's introduction to science and at the same time provides a healthy outdoor type of exercise program.

The indoor portion of a child's' schooling is designed to train the child to think for himself. This begins with the children listening to fantasy stories which require them to visualize and use their own imaginations. Imagination is even more powerful than knowledge when it comes to creativity. Then as children learn to read, they continue stories of this type and are limited to the amount of visual information they are allowed to watch since this retards the imagination process.

Starting immediately in this early period, children are taught from their stories as to what is considered right and what is considered wrong in our society. Developing good morals is much easier to do early in life and helps later to understand our rules and law. It works.

During the remainder of the initial eight years of the learning process, all children are taught the basics together. This includes not only math, science, reading and writing skills, but also subjects to improve physical skills. This includes using simple tools for carpentry and metalwork, and an introduction to the arts including musical instruments, singing, dancing, and painting.

After completing the eight years of schooling, the child or individual is then required to advance through school at his own capability rate. All subjects are taught in much greater detail. For example the "arts" which are needed to develop more creativity in an individual, rarely come naturally and must be taught. To really enjoy and appreciate any type of art, one must understand the small details that make up the art including its history and composition. This is true not only for paintings, but also for poetry, music, literature, and the visuals. The more you know of a subject, the more you can enjoy it. In the case of literature, you can not only enjoy it, but it teaches compassion. By reading current literature, you can learn about all types of people, their problems, and their life styles. A strong background in literature is required for various leadership positions in our society.

At this time new subjects are taught. History is introduced for the first time. All history is not discussed since it has been shown that in the past, grudges and prejudices tend to be perpetuated by the losers of various conflicts. This type of history, along with crimes and violence, are not taught to the student. There are enough good ideas to develop in an individuals mind, let alone introduce bad ones. If however an individual later specializes in the subject of history, all historic records are available for study and history specialists are always consulted to help with decisions on new situations. History is not lost, but details of bad influential history remains only in records.

Philosophy is taught to students as they get older, have more knowledge, and develop the capability of reasoning. This subject remains with you throughout life since you have to cultivate your mind to know yourself. Ancient religions are discussed for the first time so that an individual can better understand history and human reasoning.

The final two subjects I will mention here are the most important to one's self well being. They are meditation and self hypnosis. Originally these subjects were considered novelties by the people, but as their usefulness proved essential in the modern world, they became required subjects for older students. Self hypnosis proved to be the best technique of maintaining body control. Its ability to eliminate pain and sickness accomplished more to extending a healthy lifetime than any artificial medication. Meditation accomplished the same for the mind in that it can remove a bodies stress and cleanse the brain permitting it to function at maximum capacity with perfect memory. This is especially important as one ages.

Of course nobody can learn everything, so after twelve years of schooling, a student begins to specialize in a given field by taking courses one half of the day, and working in a related job the other half of the day. This can go on indefinitely since school time and work time are credited equally for all government benefits. Schooling and work do not conflict with one another since a student progresses at his own rate and is not required to do schoolwork out of classes from the 12th year on.

Advancement in school is based on standard unbiased testing. When a student feels he understands a given subject, he takes an oral exam before a board of individuals that are expert in the subject. This testing eliminates possible cheating and guarantees the student has full knowledge of the subject. The student can continue until he has advanced so far that there is no-one more knowledgeable to teach or test him. This is considered the top of his field. Each field has a small group of these top achievers, and they are considered the leaders of such specialized fields as food, science, medicine, education, environment, philosophy, etc.

This system of advancement in education allows a student to proceed as far as he wants, in the field for which he is best qualified. If the student is poor in higher mathematics, he can avoid the subject by going into a field such as law or social work and still proceed to the top of those fields. The same is true in the field of science where a student may have trouble or a lack of interest in the subject of history. Everyone is given the opportunity to achieve ones' maximum capability or desire.

There are many individuals however, who are satisfied to work at lower job levels and enjoy life without advanced education. In fact most people put some limit on knowledge. A good example of this is when some students still in their first twelve years of schooling have difficulty with math. Those with more analytical capability continue with advanced math, while others are taught to use computers. Computers save considerable time for routine calculating and store an infinite amount of information, but they slow down the creative process in an individual. Although children can be taught to manipulate a computer at an early age, computers are avoided as long as possible to force a child to think for himself. This is something a computer cannot do. Don't forget the people that originally designed the computer, did not have computers themselves. Of course everyone eventually is given the opportunity to learn to operate computers in order to provide more efficiency in the workplace.

So one then asks, what does a lifetime of study and education accomplish? The answer is — in our society — everything. As your education increases, you move up the job ladder. The individual who advances to the top of his field is chosen to represent the people on one of the governments decision making committees. There are seven of these specialized committees which are needed to run the nation. Each will be covered in more detail later. The highest level of achievement is to be selected as the leader of one of these seven committees. The seven individuals chosen for these positions are selected because of their knowledge in their fields of specialty, plus their understanding and added training in philosophy. This is because a true philosopher is "a lover of wisdom". In early times, philosophers contributed very little to society and just taught others or perpetuated themselves by analyzing the contribution of others. This overflow of knowledge, however, actually puts one in a better position to make decisions which are the best for the people. These decisions are made not only because they are technically correct, but because they are also right based on historical data. This is what the philosopher-specialist is capable of doing.

Although there is much personal satisfaction to being a leader in your field of specialization, the real satisfaction is achieved all through ones lifetime through personal creativity. This does not necessarily mean a major scientific breakthrough, but can, for instance, just be simple improvements in the area of farming or growing techniques. This creativity or coming up with new ideas, is always one of the most gratifying feelings an individual experiences. Although new ideas appear to come from space, they actually can only be created from the "data base" in ones' mind that has been established from learning and experience.

Personal achievement through leadership and creativity, along with peace of mind through meditation, all contribute to establishing an individuals place in society. Maximum performance in all these traits is achieved through proper and continuous education. The more you learn and know, the less you physically want or need. Individual materialism disappears. Total equality can be achieved with education for everyone and a proper government.

GOVERNMENT AND THE LAW

44*420.   *Over the centuries many men have made suggestions as to what would be needed to establish the ideal government and society.* Fortunately for us, we could look back and avoid past mistakes thereby allowing us to achieve this perfect state. Of course nothing is perfect since something perfect cannot be improved. This would mean no new ideas or changes and life would get boring. But the satisfaction with what we have achieved is close enough to perfect in that suggesting changes is very difficult.

When our ancestors originally came here, they had the advantage of being the only advanced humans on this planet. This provided the ideal conditions that allowed them to establish the perfect society. Being the new and the only civilization, meant that there was no other competing civilization to be concerned with and we did not have to feel our lifestyle was threatened by outsiders. Also having total access to the natural resources on this planet meant we were self sufficient and did not have to rely on others. If some resource were not available, it was our own fault and we would have to redefine our needs. Unlimited space was also a big advantage in that it would allow for any required expansion, and also provide isolated areas for storage of any excess, including undesirable individuals. But the most important advantage to our new society was that we knew from history our past failures and did not have to repeat them.

History of our great ancestors on our old planet, shows us that they first attempted to rule by strength, such as generally observed in the animal kingdom. Greed and the lust for power of relatively small civil or religious groups always resulted in wars and there is nothing more wasteful than war. Besides the unnecessary loss of life, there is also a large drain on the economy and its natural resources. It requires the build up of new weapons of war to guarantee survival from your enemy and at the same time a realization that none of this build up is of any benefit to the people unless there is a war. The threat of war just invites war.

Our ancestors then changed from a government of strong ruling groups and individuals to a democratic type of government. The theory was that the people knew what's best for themselves. They elected their local representatives to form the government and it resulted in total inefficiency. Those candidates most popular with the people were elected regardless of their education if any. Once elected, the main concern of the representative was to be re-elected and this did not allow him to make decisions for the overall good of all the people.

No matter what was tried, it didn't work. When the first democracy ruled, the majority tended to suppress the minority. Then the majority changed the laws to benefit and protect the minority but, in so doing, it controlled the direction of the minority and made them passive. In fact, one way to control a group of people is to make them dependent on you. This was true early in our peoples' history when slaves were originally given their freedom. Without education they were dependent on welfare and, therefore, just became slaves of the government.

In the final phases of democracy, the government attempted to redistribute the wealth by taking from the rich and giving it to the poor. This, too, was a total disaster because the lack of investments from the wealthy tended to eliminate the middle class by reducing jobs and wages. So what did we learn from historical records?

We learned that establishing a close knit united society depended on people having two needs satisfied, the need to survive and the need to be equal. The primary purpose and function of government is to fulfill these two needs. Survival and individual equality. By doing this, the government gives individuals the opportunity to achieve their goals in life which in turn provides them with happiness. Every individual should have the right to pursue happiness.

A well organized government that has access to all natural resources and controls production, has the capability of protecting and providing all of man's physical and material needs. This satisfies man's survival need. But to achieve happiness, all men must first achieve equality. The goal of equality, therefore, is the first consideration in every action the government takes. All people begin equal and must remain equal in all respects in order to keep friendships and to have peace. Is it possible for one society to serve the needs of all its citizens? The answer is yes only if the citizens of that society are under one jurisdiction and are willing to give up some of their liberties and work within the rules of that society.

When our ancestors first came to this planet, they had the advantage of a common language and the technical capability of instant communication. This minimized confusion caused by isolation and misunderstanding, and was foremost in establishing a society aimed at equality. Our government also realized that it takes more than just giving the people the same rights or privileges to make them equal. To avoid social conflicts and domination, there must be no privileged class and all forms of class distinction must be eliminated. This led to the most drastic change to our way of living, which was the elimination of money and personal ownership of property. Money or bartering is needed in a divided world, and once ownership is established in a civilization, it is almost impossible to change. In a society that uses money, individuals never seem to have enough money. The more they have, the more they want. But our ancestors were beginning with no established rules and a unified world, therefore they could do whatever they wanted.

The elimination of money resulted in the elimination of many job classifications. This included those involved with banking, finances, sales, marketing, payroll, tax collecting, cashiers, markets, and to some extent the reduction in other areas such as law. After all what would one person sue another for if it were not for money or personal gain of property? Using justice for revenge was eliminated.

With the loss of these job categories, there was a large increase in the number of people now available to produce the material goods needed for all individuals. In fact, with modern technology, all goods needed could be produced with the large available labor force and an individual still had at least half of his time to pursue his own personal endeavors.

The task of a world government needed to solve world problems is too large for any single individual to be in control. The organization of our world government, therefore, consisted of coordinating seven specialized committees. These committees were Manufacturing, Services, Education, Environment, Science (includes health), Arts, and Judicial. The leaders of each of these committees would meet periodically to discuss their needs and to establish world policies. The leader of the Judicial Committee would coordinate the meetings.

To be on one of these government committees, an individual is not elected by the people, but is selected by each committee based on his level of education and specialization in that particular field. Only the best are chosen for these jobs, and it is considered to be an honor in a position to do the most good for the most people. Once on a committee, the individual serves a short apprenticeship where he studies local conditions throughout the world in his specialty. This permits him to make the least biased decisions. A committee member does not make a decision about something he does not understand and must observe the total problem not its unrelated parts. Decisions and rulings are made by reason and what is right, not by law or personal gain.

Our world government has the advantage in that it is working with committee members who are all equal and are regulating a people having the same status. Governments of the past have always been corrupt. It was natural for a man to desire and value his own possessions and this would lead him to make decisions based on personal gain. Wealth corrupts governments. In our present world, without money or personal property, government leaders have nothing to gain by not making whatever they consider to be the best decisions. Let me now give you a short description of each of the seven committees:

1. It is the function of the Manufacturing Committee to provide and distribute the material needed by each individual in the society. These include housing, clothing, food, fuel, and even non-critical items such as those used for hobbies and recreation. Manufacturing is also responsible for the construction of roads, buildings, and the equipment used with public facilities.

2. Non-material needs of an individual are just as important as the material needs. The Services Committee maintains the work force that fulfills all of these other needs. These needs are fulfilled by services such as transportation, recreation and entertainment areas, personal grooming, nurturing, and the maintenance of all public and individual hardware and facilities.

3. The Education Committee is responsible for providing a lifelong learning program that permits each individual to achieve his maximum level of capability and creativity. This includes providing all necessary courses, testing each individual's capabilities, and keeping each a file of each individual's level of achievement. This record is most important because it determines what type of work an individual does in society and for what position he is permitted to compete. As previously mentioned, getting an education is the responsibility of each individual, but it is the government's responsibility to provide everything needed to achieve that education and to do so with an unbiased program.

4. Since the physical makeup of the planet actually controls and puts limits on society, it is the duty of the Environmental Committee to keep the balance between the environment and the needs of the people. The elements for human survival and the materials needed for manufactured goods are in limited supply on this planet. For this reason, the Environmental Committee determines how much world pollution is allowable, what must be recycled, and what natural resources are available for food and manufacturing. From this the committee determines what

limits to put on population growth.

5. The Science Committee regulates all activities related to science. This includes securing the necessary manpower to study new ideas in basic science, physics, biology, and areas related to nature and our environment. This committee is also responsible for the health of the people by setting routines for both mind and body maintenance.

6. The Arts require a special committee because of their importance to the advancement of culture and the joy they can provide for individuals. Both high and low forms of art are monitored by this committee. They include literature, painting, sculpture, music, dancing, visuals, verbals, and drama. The committee is responsible for discovering and employing the most talented individuals in all of these fields. It also is responsible for presenting classes in the education program so that all individuals develop an appreciation of all the arts. To get the most out of any art field, one must know its history, its construction, and its purpose. The more one knows about art, the more one enjoys it. Without understanding, there can be no appreciation.

7. The Judicial Committee is responsible for making judgments pertaining to "The Credenda" and for enforcing the rules. Over the centuries, thousands of laws were written to such an extreme that eventually the actions of an individual were not as important as the excuses for those actions. As a result, there was always some law in the complex web of laws that justified ignoring another law. The people finally threw out all old existing laws for the overall good. They then established the prime belief and doctrine known as "The Credenda" which is stated in one

sentence: <u>Enjoy Life To Its Fullest And Permit Others To Do The Same.</u> This single statement combines the primary reason as to what individuals are to accomplish while on this planet, and at the same time what restriction is placed on achieving that goal. It is a combination of philosophy and law, and is interpreted as giving every individual the right to protect his own freedom and avoid being put under the will and power of another individual. The old rule of reciprocity which stated that an individual could only do to others what he would allow to be done to himself was unacceptable. This is because it gave legal control to the individual taking the action over the individual being acted upon. For example, the individual who enjoys pain or combat should not have the right to inflict it on others.

It was found that with the elimination of money, and with the government essentially providing for all of the material and survival needs of its people, society was basically good. Without an abundance of laws, there was no way of breaking them. There had to be rules, however, to protect the people and to insure their contribution to society. For example, which side of a dock should a craft approach to avoid collision, or how many hours to work to receive credits for government provided necessities. All of these rules are established by the Judicial Committee only after they have been tested, shown to meet world goals, and do not infringe on individual equality.

Of course, there are always exceptions to rules, and rules are quite often broken. When this occurs, a judge or decision maker determines what action to take. Judges are individuals who have achieved the highest level of education in their fields and have strong backgrounds in philosophy. They judge by reason and the belief that human affairs should be governed by ethical principles and not by tradition, divine revelation, or manmade laws. Each case stands by itself and is judged on its own merit.

The breaking of a rule is generally not serious and results in some minor penalty such as a warning or added work detail to obtain one's credits for material allocations. If, however, an individual does not comply to "The Credenda", serious penalties are applied. An example of such a case would be when an individual physically harms another individual. A case such as this would be presented before three experienced professional judges who determine the outcome of the case based on reason and facts obtained by accurate truth monitors. History shows us that when untrained individuals from unrelated fields are used to judge the innocence or guilt of another individual, facts are secondary to emotions. Because of this, professional judges are now used in order to reach more accurate case verdicts.

Penalties for violating "The Credenda" have changed since our arrival on this planet. On our old planet, prisons were eliminated centuries ago. Guilty individuals were forced to perform the hardest and most undesirable jobs required by our civilization. If need be, mind controlling drugs would be used to sedate these individuals to remove any threat to our society. If this did not work or the crime was too serious, the individual was terminated by non-painful means.

Because of all the extra room on this planet, a more humane approach is now used. The guilty individual is given a choice of voluntarily doing his work penalty or being banished from our society and taken off our island to be on his own. Individuals who in the past would have been terminated are also given this choice. In the early years very few individuals managed to survive off our island because of the lack of modern medicines and tools. But as the centuries have progressed, small settlements in the wilderness have been established by these individuals. We monitor these settlements very closely as a study of how primitive man survived. In fact, I personally was on one of these data gathering missions when the present disaster occurred.

The government I have been describing to you is understandably large because of the major role it takes in the operation of our society. It is a much larger government than one in a money-dominated society. It controls the education of the people, regulates their jobs, provides for their needs, and advances science and the arts. It does all of this while enforcing "The Credenda" and the rules with its standing judicial force and justice system. Obeying "The Credenda" starts early in life by teaching children what is right and what is expected of them.

The difficulty with this government, as with any society, is that conformity tends to be its greatest virtue, and it is this conformity of individuals that threatens the survival of the government. This must be avoided. There are always those individuals who are willing to work, go strictly by the rules, and are happy just to be left alone. While these individuals are needed to contribute to society, they do little to advance it. Those few special, creative individuals who question every aspect of society and want something very much, are the ones who make the most contributions to society. Deviance from the norm is almost a requirement to be creative. These freedoms of thought and suggestion are needed for progress and are strongly encouraged as long as one stays within the rules of society.

The government must also realize that although its society is made up of individuals, it must unite them in a commitment to a culture of respect, justice, and peace. The peace of a society cannot be kept by force. It is in the minds of the people. In order to get people to respond to any situation, there must be solidarity or the "we" principle. People tend to ignore "others", but are quite willing to help their own group known as "we." This is why total equality is so important. Without discrimination, everyone becomes "we" so everyone deserves the help needed regardless of who they are or where they are.

Since we are all interdependent, our equality requires personal responsibilities. Every individual is responsible and accountable for his own actions. This means not blaming others for one's shortcomings. At the same time one cannot accept someone else's responsibilities since it will put them in debt to you, thereby nullifying their equality. Remember that everyone has the same individual rights which means one cannot infringe on another's individual rights. In other words, just live by "The Credenda".

Every individual is judged by his own accomplishments and not by those of his ancestors. One does not inherit a title or position, and at the same time is not responsible for any inappropriate act a former generation may have performed. One now lives in the present and forgets the past. History has shown us that hate and prejudice passed down from one generation to the next will result in continued feuds and even wars.

In summary, we can say that the government is organized to support "The Credenda" by providing its people with security and equality. At the same time, all individuals have an agreement with the government to give up some of their freedom for the benefits they are provided. The people must realize there is more to a thriving society than just being good and obeying the rules. Otherwise, what has one accomplished in life? Every individual must make an effort to educate himself and to develop his personal skills to the highest level. This then allows that individual to create and contribute the most to society.

SCIENCE, NATURE AND HEALTH

45*453. Almost all of the great improvements in society have been made through advancements in science and technology making them the controlling factor of our lives. Science is based not on assumptions, but on the truth and facts that are derived from the general laws of nature, with nature being neither good nor bad - just nature. Nature has proved that it is self regulating and requires no divine overseer, but as man's knowledge of the wonders of the universe increases, some still wonder if God and nature are one in the same.

Trying to understand the universe is a continuing goal of science. The power of the human mind has linked the Earth with the heavens to demonstrate it can understand the workings of nature and man. We still do not know why the laws of nature and physics work as they do, but we have learned what they are and how they are defined. There is no such thing as a "complete unified theory" that explains everything about the universe. There are just lots of theories that, when combined, describe it more accurately.

When it comes to science and nature, there is nothing more important than the environment we live in. Man must learn all he can about nature, good or bad, and then utilize it as best he can. In early times, man was totally dominated by nature and had to adapt to existing conditions for survival. This meant the eating of local vegetation and animals, using available shelter such as caves and trees, and living near water for both drink and eventual transportation. But man's ability to think and develop tools separated him from other species. He became not just a figure in the landscape, but a shaper of that landscape. As man's knowledge of science and physics increased, so did his control over nature. This resulted in technological improvements with the most advanced societies always having dominance over a static society.

Man has come to realize that all wealth comes from nature and the environment, so it is important not to destroy it. Ask yourself how long it takes to replace a tree once it has been destroyed by fire. Basic materials such as metal, wood, and fuels, are all limited in supply and must, therefore, be conserved and recycled. They are needed to advance society. Our fate and happiness depends on our ability to co-exist with nature as it exists on our planet. We have to be concerned with the future because that is where we are going to spend the rest of our lives and you can't stop the future from coming.

There is no better example of mans' dependence on nature than the subject of environmental pollution. By observing our planet from outer space, one can see just how thin and fragile our atmosphere is. The environment we depend on for our survival is less than 10 units in thickness over the surface of this entire planet. This thin layer includes the food we eat, the water we drink, the air we breathe, and the protection it provides us from the rest of the universe. When we make any change to this environment, we are conducting an experiment on ourselves which ultimately effects our health, safety, and welfare. Our study of the universe had shown that, within practical travel limits from our planet, there are only two existing locations where a similar environment exists. This allowed for a pos-sible evacuation from this planet, if necessary, but now with the loss of our advanced civilization and means of travel, man has to survive here and conserve what he has.

Man's dependence on the environment dates back to when the universe was formed. Everything in the universe is made of the same materials including man. In fact you can say man is made of star dust and is a world in minia-ture. His cells are made of molecules controlled by energy fields. Life is a progression passed down from individual to individual through living cells and is not newly created every time an individual is born. Life is always in the process of changing to something else and change is always gradual.

The universe operates by natural selection and not by a fixed design. Species that best adapt to the outside envi-ronment in which they live are the ones that survive on their own. This is true not only of man, but of all plants and animals. But since man now has the power to control or destroy other species, it is his duty to help others to survive. How dull the world would be if only one or two other animal varieties existed.

When our ancestors first came here from our old planet, their bodies had to adapt to their new environment. These changes took place over many generations, but fortunately, the changes were small because this planet was similar to our old one. Changes in their bone structure because of less gravity, and adjusting their bodies time to changes in lightness and darkness because of the planet's rotation, were made without complications. What proved to be the most important environmental factor, was the location of the sun relative to this planet. This location was selected because it provided our ancestors the same temperature they were used to living in. It is the sun that sustains life by providing every bit of our energy, and it can be said that its rays are the magic stuff of life itself. All plants and animals that have evolved on this planet, need the sun to survive.

In no other field has science made a larger contribution than in the development and health of man himself. Through gene cleansing, an individual starts life in perfect health when first born. This perfect health is maintained throughout one's lifetime with the large selection of drugs that have become available over the centuries to control disease and abnormalities. Even aging has been slowed down by modifying the genetic aging clock within our cells thereby giving us the ability to greatly reproduce our blood cells, skin, bones, etc. The average individual ages very slowly and typically lives 150 years in our present civilization.

But mans' greatest improvement comes from the use and understanding of his brain. Without it man would just be another animal roaming the planet and waiting for his extinction. One must realize that the body does not develop the brain, but the brain develops the body. Your mind is in every cell of your body and this is what allows you to control your own body. The mind is not only a place to store knowledge for creative purposes, but when properly used is the biggest factor in maintaining an individual's good health. Stress, depression, and pain, can be completely eliminated with proper mind control. Healing of the body, controlling one's blood flow, and preventing some diseases with a healthy mind, are all within an individual's own control. The mind is a medication for good health.

To achieve this ultimate mind control requires continuous practice. As one ages, there are brain cleansing medications available to thin or remove old coatings, thereby permitting a perfect memory and a brain that works at maximum capacity. But throughout life, body control is only accomplished through deep meditation. Children are taught meditation early in life and it becomes part of everyone's daily regimentation.

Besides controlling one's health, the mind is also responsible for how creative an individual is, and in today's modern society, creativity ranks number one in achieving self satisfaction. When a person with a creative mind discovers a new technique or phenomenon, he immediately tries to think of using it for a new application. The key word here is to think. The individual must somehow contact his subconscious or "higher self" to apply this newly acquired knowledge with the knowledge already stored in his mind. Although new ideas appear to come from space, they actually come from knowledge analyzed through the thought process. This combination of new knowledge with the old knowledge that was obtained through schooling and experience, is what is needed for the creative process. The product that results from this creative process is what separates one individual from another, allowing him to make his contribution to immorality. The afterlife of any individual only lasts as long as that individual's thoughts and deeds are remembered by future generations.

Although creativity exists in all fields of endeavor, it is most obviously noted in the scientific field. This is primarily due to the fact that new scientific discoveries result in applications that can quickly contribute to mankind's materialistic use. The universe was not made solely for our use, so it is up to us to develop and make it the best we can for ourselves. Although scientific knowledge tells us what can be done, it is man that decides what should be done. This control by man must not only be just and moral, but must also be well thought out. A good example of this was the advancement of nourishment in the field of health.

Man's desire at one time was to develop a "food pill" that could replace hunger and starvation, thereby simplifying space travel and giving an individual more personal time by not having to cook or eat. A pill was finally developed and appeared successful in that it provided a complete diet, controlled fat and weight, and, with a little exercise, a person could keep his muscles in shape. What was over-looked was that man's body slowly changed and adapted to this new life style. Meats and vegetables were no longer eaten and man's waste and digestive system could no longer handle these foods. These individuals could not live directly off the land, and those most converted to the "food pill" style of life, soon became the weakest and least likely to survive by themselves. They became dependent on society and modern technology to provide the needed pills. For these reasons and the desire for man's survival, diets using only "food pills" were abandoned.

One more example of controlling scientific progress from a practical level is that of atom modification. By restructuring atoms, man now has the capability of an unlimited supply of any element. Gold for example, which is difficult to find in large quantities in nature, can now be readily manufactured. Unfortunately, this restructuring process does require large amounts of energy so that decisions must be made as to which applications this process should be used for. Today it is almost entirely used to optimize metals that provide near perfect conduction for both heat and electrical energy. These superconducting metals are the most needed materials in the advanced technological world. I should also mention that the potential of this atom modification process to produce materials for destructive weapons has always been known, yet it has never been used for that application.

To close this short discussion on science and nature, I would like to do a little personal rambling. All of my life I have been somehow involved in the scientific field and I still find each day more fascinating than the previous one. Whenever I encounter a problem, I realize there is an unknown, and this challenge is what makes the present so much more interesting than the past.

By just sitting here on this beach I can gaze at the night sky and see things such as distant galaxies that man will never reach. I realize that the light emitted from these galaxies happened millions of years ago permitting me to look back in time. Yet I've also learned it is impossible for me to go back in time or else locations such as this planet would exist forever.

We are taught the thrill of discovery early in our childhood. Just digging a hole in the ground was fun because you didn't know what you would find. We were taught that the world is full of new discoveries made every day and the importance of these discoveries determines if they should be shared with others, or kept for personal enjoyment. Just picture a child sitting in a field and discovering a flower or an insect crawling on the ground that will probably never be seen by another human. Such beauty and discovery surrounds everyone every day and must be appreciated.

Under normal conditions, matter cannot be created or destroyed. To me that means I am made of particles that were here billions of years ago and it took that long to create me. My existence is the result of millions of events and processes that finally resulted in my birth. Besides my physical characteristics, my unique senses and talent for numbers and music have been passed down to me from a chain of previous lifetimes. Of course, this does not mean that others not inheriting these talents cannot develop them on their own, it just makes it easier for those possessing the genes to develop them if they make the effort.

All newly born babies begin life as a mass of related genes. As a baby it has an open mind with certain innate desires and cell memories that must be developed. This development is based on experience, education, and mind search; and continues throughout one's lifetime. Much of your sensory information is passed down through your genes to future generations who must then discover these talents on their own and add to them. Of course when an individual dies, life as we know it ceases and his unique chain of genes comes to an end.

All of this is what makes my present life so special to me. I have no remembrance of the billions of years it took to create me, and I have no idea what my remains will create in the future once my body decomposes. What is important

to me is to realize I am unique and now is the time everything has come together to form me. It is the present that
every individual should enjoy and partake in since no one
knows what the universe has in store for them in the
future.

SOCIAL LIFE, MATING AND WORK

46*492. *As mentioned before, the goal of our government is to promote individual equality.* To accomplish this, the government provides for the same basic needs in all individuals in exchange for a required amount of work performed throughout one's lifetime. Although this work at first appears to be a limit to an individual's independence, it is necessary so that the government may perform its function. At the same time this work is accepted by the people knowing everyone is contributing to society.

Some of the basics provided to each individual include food, shelter, clothing, fuel, and personal services such as health care and recreational facilities. Shelter, for example, can be separate units or multiple living quarters depending on an individual's choice. These units are all self sustaining, requiring little maintenance. They have such conveniences as a dust free atmosphere, total waste recycling, and a self contained energy system that provides all the required heat and light. Even individual water makers are included to store the needed water for each unit.

To promote individuality, everyone is given a choice as to what food they eat, the clothing they wear, their transportation, and all other materialistic items. As long as each individual achieves his required work credits, any personal item can be obtained by simply requesting it. No money is required in our society. Since everyone can fill material needs by simply making a request, a major step towards individual equality has been achieved. Without the need for money or private ownership, competition between materialistic individuals was eliminated. It has been shown that when an individual can have everything he wants, he no longer has the desire to have everything. In fact, in our society, having fewer needs demonstrates greater individual independence and people do not live in material excess.

The question then becomes — what do people want if they have everything? The answer has to be "nothing" with respect to materialistic needs. What is important is that man take advantage of the time allotted for his life span and to keep from getting bored. To stay happy and healthy, it is important to keep both the mind and body busy.

Almost every day involves work and/or some form of education; along with personal time for play, socializing, physical exercise, relaxation, and rejuvenation. An individual's aggressive tendencies are channeled to sports and physical activities just as they have been over the centuries. For relaxation, however, many new techniques have been developed that continue to improve the full potential of the mind while resting and meditating. The most interesting and enjoyable of these is being able to control one's dreams while resting, and to perform mind travel while meditating.

With proper training and practice, an individual can develop the ability to transpose himself into an outside experience. With the mind, it is possible to picture one self in any location or situation and actually to control the body's senses to see, taste, smell, hear, and feel the experience. This type of meditation is taught in school and uses the same body and mind controlling techniques that are used for controlling one's own health. In early civilizations, man used mind altering drugs and machines to accomplish these activities, but now this can be accomplished through aggressive mind training. I should mention, though, that even with all these physical and mind entertaining activities, individuals still sometimes find that doing simply nothing is a good solution for rest and relaxation.

With the ability to control one's own body and needs, an individual is another step closer to independence and equality. The goal is not having to rely on someone else for your survival or welfare. A baby relying on its parents for survival or, as history shows, a wife relying on a husband to meet her needs, are both examples where one party has control or domination over another. Obviously if someone is dependent on someone else, they themselves are not independent and lose their freedom. Of course these types of situations also act as a double edged sword. No individual can really be independent if another individual is dependent upon them. The true test of independence is having the ability and freedom to walk away from any given situation. This brings us to a subject that played a major part in early civilizations — marriage and families.

When man first came into existence, he was able to dominate the female simply with his strength. As time passed, the role of the female remained dependent on the male to provide for survival, while she performed the domesticated role of taking care of the family's children. This relationship lasted many centuries until equality in education finally brought it to an end. Education resulted in male-female equality by allowing the female to gain her independence with the ability to provide for herself. Once a female could handle her own survival and security, there was really no need for marriage or a husband. Let's list the reasons why couples at one time considered marriage a necessity, and discuss why in today's world it no longer applies. The reasons for marriage were as follows:

1. Security
2. State laws and estates
3. Religious reasons
4. Sexual reasons
5. Love and companionship
6. Children and a family

In today's society there is no need for money, near perfect health is the norm, and the government provides for the materialistic needs of all individuals as long as the required work credits are earned. This along with any required care during one's final years, is all that is needed for an individual's security.

State laws relating to marriage have all been discontinued along with all other laws. To achieve equality, which is the goal of government, marriage cannot exist because everyone must be treated as an individual and not as a couple. Marriage requires dependence on others thereby the loss of freedom.

Family estates and inheritance have also been eliminated. Without money or private property, an estate does not exist and is not needed. All individuals are given their own names to perpetuate and do not carry a family name. This encourages personal achievement and not one that is passed down from previous ancestors. Everyone is responsible for his own status and ability.

With the elimination of organized religion, religious ceremonies and beliefs related to marriage are no longer in existence.

The purpose of engaging in sex is solely for enjoyment and should not be limited only to those who are married. It should be obvious that if a woman has sexual relations only once or twice in her lifetime for the purpose of having a child, 99% of the time sex serves a different purpose. It can be for personal enjoyment and satisfaction, or a means of sharing or giving to a close partner. It definitely is needed to maintain the best of health by keeping the body functioning properly. With sexual diseases being eliminated many years ago, and with the government now regulating birth control, all sexual relationships are now considered safe.

In today's world sexual freedom is socially acceptable. There are locations specifically designed to meet partners for engaging in sex, but at all times everyone must abide by "The Credenda" which allows anyone not to participate by simply refusing. Not everyone needs a specific partner and one may choose a life style to participate at these locations for many years.

Although unlimited sex and variety may be a great form of pleasure and entertainment early in life, almost all individuals find a single partner that they would like to spend most of their time with to share love and companionship. We have found that marriage is not necessary to keep two individuals together and that most do it for a lifetime. When both parties realize that either of them has the freedom to leave at any time, those truly in love can always find common grounds to stay together. In fact, more couples stay together now than history shows of married couples in the past.

This brings us to the last and strongest argument for marriage, that of having children and a family. Many years ago it was demonstrated that babies could be brought into the world using artificial life support systems. One man can produce many sperms and one woman can produce many eggs. These can all be used to produce new babies. Fortunately, our leaders realized that utilization of this method of birth production could result in women losing their ability to perform child births on their own because of evolution and gene change. Since children are needed for survival of the human race, birth by artificial means was banned.

The government is now totally in charge of population growth. The Environmental Committee determines the allowable annual births from inputs by the other committees and the needs of the people. Can our manufacturing and service groups provide all of our peoples needs? How much food supply is projected to be available, and are we pushing the limits of the natural resources in our environment? All these questions must be answered.

Next is the selection of which couples are to be used to produce the children. In today's world, all individuals are inoculated early in life to prevent unscheduled or unwanted children. This can be reversed thereby permitting only those couples wanting children to have them. Many individuals and couples are happy throughout life without having children and prefer the greater sense of freedom. Fortunately, they have this control and choice.

Couples must be between the ages of 25 and 50 to be selected for progenitive status. Research has shown that children born to parents in this age range grow up with more love, more intelligence, and a better childhood than those with younger parents. A family unit is different now than it was in the past. A child now spends most of its time away from home starting some education already at the age of three. Ten years later the child is already capable of surviving in society on its own by earning work credits with education time and minor tasks. The child's biological parents are not needed for material help and have nothing such as property or money to pass on to their children. In fact the child does not even carry a family name since, as mentioned earlier, this eliminates any inherited status and promotes equality. Fortunately, there always seem to be enough couples that think children are fun and getting them started in life is purpose enough. To them, being needed is worth the sacrifice of freedom. Those involved with having children have the added advantage of being qualified as a nurturer, and can then be selected to train and work with young children once their own children have grown up. To earn work credits in this services field requires individuals that have had children and family experience.

Controlling the population controls the labor force and it is the government's function to keep this balance. It accomplishes this by defining every job position based on the need for each position. This includes all classifications such as security, services, health, regulation, judicial, government, entertainment, the arts, and the majority of which go into education and manufacturing. The public demand for each of these functions determines how jobs are distributed.

Each job position is defined by the level of education and physical requirements needed. The position is then filled based only on these two requirements. Gender, age, and even the name of the applicant are not considered. Ability, not social standing, is what counts. This selection system shows one of the advantages of continuing higher education. Obviously, the more education one has, the more jobs there are to choose from, and the higher the position one can apply for. Education is available to everyone at any age so they can improve themselves, but everyone is not fitted for continuous education. Some individuals reach their learning limits, while others are happy with the jobs they have and just wish to enjoy life as it is. After all, the government provides their material needs as long as they are working.

Let me explain what work credits are since I have mentioned them several times in these discussions. Each individual is given "credits" for time spent working or getting an education. As long as an individual accrues the minimum number of credits required, he or she is provided with all food and materialistic requests. The minimum number of credits needed is approximately a half day of work or education, although less time is required later in life since that time is considered more valuable. Those individuals not meeting their minimum requirements, or those found trying to take advantage of other workers' efforts, are penalized. They along with others found breaking society's rules, are assigned those jobs in the community that have not been applied for, or are menial and undesirable. If they do not perform their penalized jobs, their banishment is considered. In some respects this action may sound severe, but people in today's society realize all good things come from effort. Nothing comes from nothing.

To have a perfect society, everyone has to agree to have that society. There is no place for those who won't contribute. When this society was formed, many people still remembered the way it originally was. Back then, the sole purpose of life was to make a living. Company owners and their laborers were on opposite ends. The owners were generally greedy making money and not having society as their primary concern. Labor tried to fight back by organizing its people but failed because it treated each laborer equally with longevity as the way towards advancement. Since skill and education had little value, gifted and creative individuals were held back. This weakened the labor force and it just became another machine.

Today, more and more production is done with less people. Machines have eliminated muscle power and efficiency and productivity have soared. The results has been a surplus of labor which is called profit, not unemployment. Since there is no concern for money or private property, government can utilize this excess labor to eliminate scarcity and provide products and services for everyone. It has taken a long time, but with proper control, all people can now have their needs provided. This includes not only food and shelter, but their individual desires for such things as transportation, travel, recreation, and other personal interests within limits. Once the government finally caught up on the personal requests of individuals, future demands were filled in short order.

In this state of near paradise, people do not mind working at their jobs and have many different assignments throughout their lifetime. They realize they have the opportunity through available education to further improve their position, or they can just relax and work at the job level for which they are qualified. Either way they will continue to receive full benefits from the government. This holds true even for older individuals as they approach the limits of their lifespan and find themselves incapable of keeping to a routine work schedule. The government continues to provide for these elderly.

Although manufacturing is only one part of society, it is the largest group and the one needing the most attention. It requires the highest level of efficiency and productivity in order to produce the goods needed and requested by everyone. This means that if demand for products should drop, it is the one group that could run out of work. For this reason the government supports a large program to create new ideas for new products to produce. When you stop to think about it, a society that has most everything, finds it very difficult to come up with new ideas or needs. This is like trying to schedule a new invention. Ancient man was content without wheels or guns because there were none and he could not envision them. The same holds true today for such items as a qua communicator or speed travel. Our people did not miss or desire these items since they never before existed. However, once available, it seems everyone desires them. Coming up with these new ideas is the way to maintain man's progress. It is also a major factor in determining the allowable population growth since our society requires a balance between providing for everyone's needs, and a work force that only works for one half of the day.

The new ideas for producing the new products relate primarily to the manufacturing group, but "creativity" relates to everyone in society. Enjoying the fruits of your labor is one of the most important needs in life, and creativity brings recognition. Honor rolls exist listing the names of individuals that have made major contributions to society. They exist in all fields including art, entertainment, education, science, manufacturing, government, and even services. Anyone demonstrating high creativity is added to these honor rolls and is then considered a major contributor to their field. There are no added benefits for this recognition other than one's name prolonging in historic records. To have your name added to the honor roll is the highest recognition for individual achievement and a definite boost in one's self satisfaction.

47*520. (restricted)

48*539. (restricted)

49*581. (restricted)

50*607. (restricted)

MAN'S GOAL IN LIFE

51*627.   *In earlier times man would picture paradise as a place where individuals were free and independent, had perfect health, and all their needs were satisfied.* All these we have achieved right here on this planet showing paradise is not a place, but a state of mind. Even in this near perfect world, there will always be some types of struggle and conflict. What life is about is how you deal with those conflicts.

The age old question of "why am I here?" is really not important at all. What is important is what you do with your life while you are here. Everyone needs a continuing goal in life to keep from getting bored. This separates man from other animals. All animals have the same routine, day after day. They wake up, eat, drink, and seek shelter to survive; and at some stage in life they reproduce. Every day serves the same purpose to life which is to survive and reproduce.

The species of man has also learned to survive and reproduce, but because of man's superior mind, he can do this while enjoying life at the same time. Everyone must live their own life and no matter how long it is, life is always too short. Every individual should ask oneself, "If I were born an adult and only had one or two weeks to live, what would I want to do?" The answer to this question will tell you what is most important in life. I guarantee the answer would not be to obtain wealth or material goods since they would make no contribution to your remaining time. Almost everyone's first choice would be to take the time to enjoy the everyday pleasures of our world. To some this might be enjoying good friends or good food, while to others it may be enjoying the simple beauty of nature from the smell of its flowers to its peaceful sunsets. If this is true, why not make this your goal everyday of your life?

As it turns out, our goal in life and the law we live by is summarized in "The Credenda" which says "Enjoy Life To Its Fullest And Permit Others To Do The Same." We should enjoy life by doing as much as we feel comfortable with but not over extending. By just getting to know yourself and enjoying the beauty of our world, a person will live a longer, healthier, and more meaningful life. The goal and purpose to life is not complex or mysterious, it is simply to enjoy it. Everything else is secondary.

A NEW BEGINNING—AN EPILOGUE

52*632. It has been over a year since the explosion obliterated Acol, and the skies are now clear. My ship is almost buried in the sand and I have made this beach my home. I have given up any hope of other survivors from Acol and all that remains of our civilization are the items on this beach and the large symbols scattered around the globe that were built thousands of years ago by our ancestors. It would be a pity if descendants from our old planet would finally arrive now that there is no one to greet them.

As far as I know, this book is the only recording of the history of my people. I chose to leave this recording in writing since if found it will eventually be understood by man. Other methods of recording such as rings and points, could be easily overlooked because of their small size and the advanced technology needed to use and recognize them.

To the best of our knowledge and by studying the progress of the primitive settlements located on this planet, it will take another 10,000 years to recycle civilization and return it to its peak intelligence and ultimate society. I have had the opportunity to observe this planet and realize that even though beings of superior intelligence began its establishment, there is again the need to start all over. Once more the planet is covered with nomads and cave dwellers writing on the walls and again starting new religions to explain the unknowns. Fortunately this planet still has a long life and this is just another beginning to the cycle of civilization

Good Luck,

NATLOZ